Dear Parent:
Your child's love of reading starts here!

Every child learns to read in a different way and at his or her own speed. Some go back and forth between reading levels and read favorite books again and again. Others read through each level in order. You can help your young reader improve and become more confident by encouraging his or her own interests and abilities. From books your child reads with you to the first books he or she reads alone, there are I Can Read Books for every stage of reading:

SHARED READING
Basic language, word repetition, and whimsical illustrations, ideal for sharing with your emergent reader

BEGINNING READING
Short sentences, familiar words, and simple concepts for children eager to read on their own

READING WITH HELP
Engaging stories, longer sentences, and language play for developing readers

READING ALONE
Complex plots, challenging vocabulary, and high-interest topics for the independent reader

ADVANCED READING
Short paragraphs, chapters, and exciting themes for the perfect bridge to chapter books

I Can Read Books have introduced children to the joy of reading since 1957. Featuring award-winning authors and illustrators and a fabulous cast of beloved characters, I Can Read Books set the standard for beginning readers.

A lifetime of discovery begins with the magical words "I Can Read!"

Visit www.icanread.com for information on enriching your child's reading experience.

ISBN 978-0-545-91007-1

12 11 10 9 8 7 6 5 4 3 2 1   15 16 17 18 19 20/0

Printed in the U.S.A.   40

First Scholastic printing, September 2015

Pinkalicious®

The Pinkatastic Story Collection

by Victoria Kann

SCHOLASTIC INC.

Pinkalicious®

School Rules!

by Victoria Kann

To Zelda, Grace, and David
—V.K.

The author gratefully acknowledges
the artistic and editorial contributions
of Daniel Griffo and Susan Hill.

School is okay.

Except for one thing.

When I am at school,

I miss Goldilicious.

Goldie, for short.

Goldie is my unicorn.

I really like my teacher.

His name is Mr. Pushkin.

I have some friends in my class
and I made a new friend yesterday.
But I miss Goldie anyway.

This morning when I woke up

I had a very good idea.

I could bring Goldie to school with me!

School would be
perfectly pinkatastic
with Goldilicious
there, too.

There was a shiny red apple
on Mr. Pushkin's desk.

Goldie took the apple
and nibbled it gently.

Mr. Pushkin heard Goldie munching
and he thought it was me.
"Pinkalicious, there is no eating
until snack time," he said.
"It's the rule."

"It's not me," I said.

"It's Goldilicious, my unicorn!

She didn't eat much for breakfast,"

I added.

Mr. Pushkin smiled.

He took me aside

and he told me that unicorns

are not allowed in school.

"It's the rule," he said.

Rules are something

I do not love about school.

And I really do not love

the rule about no unicorns.

I began to cry a little.

I cried a little harder.

"Okay, Pinkalicious,"

said Mr. Pushkin.

"Your unicorn may stay,

just this once."

I stopped crying.

In fact, I clapped and twirled.

"But if your unicorn stays, you must teach her the rules," Mr. Pushkin said. "Do you think you can do that?"

"Yes!" I said.

"I know I can!"

At reading time,

Goldilicious was very quiet.

Goldilicious helped me with my math.

Unicorns are very good at counting.

When it was time for recess,

I showed Goldilicious

how to line up by the door.

Goldilicious did not push

or wiggle or cut the line at all.

Goldilicious played nicely

with the other kids.

Everyone had so much fun
with Goldie and me.

I didn't know I had

so many friends at school!

Soon it was time to go home.

Goldie got my backpack

off its hook.

"Tell me, Pinkalicious,"

said Mr. Pushkin.

"Did you and your unicorn

have a good day?"

"We sure did!" I said.

9/0

"School rules!"

Soccer Star

by Victoria Kann

For Leigha,
my shining star!
—V.K.

The author gratefully acknowledges
the artistic and editorial contributions
of Daniel Griffo and Susan Hill.

Daddy gave me a new pink soccer ball.

That pink ball inspired me

to kick and score like never before!

I couldn't wait

to play the first game of the year.

Our team is called the Pinksters.

They are the Ravens.

"Pink soccer balls are for babies,"
said Kendra.

Tiffany said, "Pink stinks."

"Play ball!" said the coach.

"Think pink!" said Rose.

But I kept hearing Tiffany say

"Pink stinks."

"I'll show her pink does not stink,"

I said to Rose.

The ball came to me.

I kicked it.

It went too short.

Next the ball went too long.

Then it went crazy.

Oops!

I kicked the ball to Tiffany

by mistake.

She scored a goal.

The score was one for them,

zero for the Pinksters.

Rose scored a goal.

"Good job, Rose!" I said.

The score was tied.

One for them, one for us,

and two minutes left to play.

Then Kendra kicked the ball.

The ball sailed up high.

I heard *Pink stinks*

inside my head.

I had to get that ball!

As I ran to the ball,

Goldilicious galloped toward me.

She scooped me up on her back.

We left the park far below.

We flew across the sky.

We saw girls playing soccer
all over the world!

We flew to the pink sands of Egypt.

I made a great pass!

I did a corner kick to Spain.

"*¡Pensar en rosa!*" a girl said to me.

That's "Think pink!" in Spanish.

Cherry blossoms bloomed in China.

The girls cheered "Think pink!"

in Chinese.

"Shi fěnhóng!"

By the time we got to Italy,

I forgot all about mean old Tiffany.

"Goldilicious, let's get back

to the game," I said.

"I've learned so much.

I think I know what to do now."

I ran.

I got the ball.

I took aim and I kicked.

I did it!

I scored!

The Pinksters won.

"Wow, good job!" said Kendra.

"Pink?" said Tiffany.

"It doesn't stink."

"Three cheers for Pinkalicious!"
said Rose.

I cheered, too.

Three cheers for pink soccer players everywhere!

Pinkie Promise

by Victoria Kann

For Marjorie and Bob,
thank you for your support and guidance.
—V.K.

The author gratefully acknowledges
the artistic and editorial contributions
of Daniel Griffo and Susan Hill.

I was making a picture
for my teacher, Mr. Pushkin.
I ran out of my favorite color.

I asked my friend Alison

if I could borrow her paints.

"Just don't use up all the pink," she said.

"I won't," I said.

"I promise."

I worked very hard on the picture.

It looked good.

I gave the picture to Mr. Pushkin.

"What a terrific painting!" he said.

"It's so pink."

"You mean it's pinkerrific!" I said.

Alison was coming over
to get her paint set.

Some of the colors were empty.

Uh-oh.

What was I going to do?

"Um . . . I'm sorry, Alison," I said.

"By mistake I used up all the pink."

Alison frowned.

"You also used up all the red

and the white," she said.

"Well, red and white make pink,

so really it's all pink," I said.

Alison was angry.

"You said you wouldn't use up
all the pink paint!" said Alison.
"You promised."
"I'm really really sorry, Alison,"
I said again.
Alison took her paint set
and walked away.

Alison did not sit with me at lunch.

I sat alone.

I ate my jelly sandwich.

Jelly does not taste pink-a-yummy

if you are eating all by yourself.

Then I thought of something.

I went back to the classroom.

I made Alison a card to apologize.

"This card is very blue,"

I said to Alison.

"There were no other colors.

Almost everybody is out of pink."

"Thanks for the card," Alison said.

"It's not just beautiful, it's bluetiful."

"Alison," I asked,

"can we still be friends?"

"Of course we're friends,
Pinkalicious," Alison said.
"I'm sorry I got angry
about the paint.
I won't get so mad next time."

84

I was so happy!

"Let's play this weekend!" I said.

When Alison came over to play,

I had a surprise for her.

I gave Alison a new tube of paint.

"It's not even my birthday!"

said Alison.

"And that's not all," I said.

"Guess what?"

We got ice cream!

We shared a pink peppermint ice cream sundae with raspberry swirl syrup.

The sundae had two cherries on top
so we could each have our own.
Some things are just too hard to share!

PLEASING POMEGRANATE PUNCH

MAGENTA MINT MANGO

PINK PEPPERMINT

PLUM PINK PERFECTION

"Let's always be friends,"
Alison said.
"Yes, that would be funtastic,"
I said.

91

"Let's make it a pinkie promise!"
we said at the same time.

"Pinkie promises last forever,"
I said happily.

Pinkalicious®
and the Pinkatastic Zoo Day

by Victoria Kann

For Megan!
xox,
Aunt Victoria

The author gratefully acknowledges
the artistic and editorial contributions
of Daniel Griffo and Natalie Engel.

One sunny Saturday,

I squeezed my teddy bear tight.

"Guess what, Henrietta," I said.

"It's Teddy Bear Day at the zoo!"

"I'm bringing Fred," said Peter.

97

At the zoo, we walked by the zebras.

"These guys could use

a hint of pink," I said to myself.

I waved my wand and pink-a-presto!
A zebra changed the color of
its stripes.

"Pink!" I waved my wand at the lions.

The hippos and rhinos came next.

"Pink! Pink!" I commanded.

"What are you doing, Pinkalicious?"

asked Peter.

I waved my wand at him, too.

Then I remembered the teddy bear picnic.

I love teddy bears and picnics!

Peter and I gave Fred and Henrietta

teddy-back rides down the path.

The Teddy Bear Day fun was starting!

We got bear-shaped balloons.

We spread out a large blanket.

We sipped honey tea

and ate teddy bear cookies.

Peter gave Fred a sip of tea, too.

"Fred says this tea is BEARY good,"

said Peter.

103

I couldn't wait to see
the real bears,
but when we got to the bears
they were all sleeping.
It was boring to watch.

"Pinkalicious!" Peter pointed.

I looked up and gasped.

Above us, a vine led from

the monkey house to a field.

One monkey was crossing over!

The little monkey

did tricks on the vine.

She swung from side to side.

She hung upside down by her tail.

I didn't want Henrietta to miss out,
so Daddy put her on his shoulder.

I saw the monkey look at Henrietta.

She clapped her hands and hooted.

I had a funny feeling that something

bad was about to happen.

"Oh, no!" I cried
as the monkey swung down low.
She scooped up Henrietta!
"Well I'll be a monkey's uncle,"
Daddy said, amazed.

I watched as the monkey
scurried over to the field.
"She thinks Henrietta is
her teddy bear," Peter said.

The monkey rocked Henrietta
and gave her a big hug.
Peter laughed.
But I didn't think it was funny.
Not one little bit.

I tried everything to get the monkey

to bring Henrietta back.

I sang to her.

I made silly faces at her.

I even asked Peter to try

speaking in monkey to her.

Nothing worked!

She kept on playing with Henrietta.

"You're making a monkey

out of my teddy bear!" I said.

"I'm sorry, Pinkalicious,"
said Mommy.
"The zoo is closing.
We have to go."

"Oh, no! This is unbearable.

What about Henrietta?" I said.

I started to cry.

"We'll think of something,"

Daddy promised.

I didn't know what else to do.

At home, all I could think about

was poor Henrietta.

I loved her so much.

How could I explain that

to a monkey?

Suddenly, I had an idea.

"Quick, Peter," I said.

I told him my plan.

We got right to work.

The next day,

we got to the zoo bright and early.

I found the little monkey right away.

"I have a gift for you," I said.

I held up the snuggly sock monkey

that Peter and I had made.

"Now watch me," I told the monkey.

I gave the new toy a squeeze.

The monkey hugged Henrietta.

I patted the sock monkey's head.

The little monkey patted Henrietta.

I tossed the sock monkey into the field.

The monkey tossed Henrietta over to me!

I picked up my teddy bear
and the little monkey
picked up her new friend.

"Good-bye!" I waved.

"It was fun monkeying around

with you!"

Pinkalicious®

The Princess of Pink
Slumber Party

by Victoria Kann

For Jennifer and Sydney
—V.K.

The author gratefully acknowledges
the artistic and editorial contributions
of Jared Osterhold and Natalie Engel.

I was having a slumber party.

It was not any old slumber party.

It was a Princess of Pink party!

My whole family got ready.

Mommy and Daddy dressed up

like a queen and a king.

"I'm the royal prince," said Peter.

He grabbed a crown out of my hand.

"You're more like a royal joker,"

I told him.

DING DONG!

"The princesses are here!" I said.

I twirled my way to the door

and let my royal friends in.

"Welcome," I said with a curtsy.

"Enter the castle, fair maidens!"

"How grand!" Molly said.

"I'm ready for the ball!" Rose said.

"Hello, Princess Alison," I said.

"Hi," Alison said quietly.

She held her bear tightly.

"Let's play musical thrones!"

I started the music

and we danced around the chairs.

I didn't even mind being

the last one left without a throne.

132

"Yay! I won!" said Molly.

"Your prize, Your Majesty," I said.

I handed Molly a pinkatastic wand.

"It's time to make tiaras!" I said.

"Ohhhh," Rose said.

"Look at the dazzling jewels!"

"My tiara is going to twinkle

like a star," said Molly.

"Look at me," I said.

I put my tiara proudly on my head.

"I have the sparkliest tiara
in all the land!"

"Dinner is served!" said Mommy.

"We made a royal feast," said Daddy.

"Princess-and-the-Split-Pea Soup,

Chicken Nuggets à la King,

and Castle Cupcakes for dessert!"

Peter said, "If I was ruler,

we'd always eat dessert first!"

"Yum," I said.

"That would be a very sweet kingdom!"

After dinner Peter climbed
to the top of a pile of pillows
and yelled, "I'm king of the castle!"

"It's princess of the castle
around here," I said.
"Princesses rule!" Molly said.

Suddenly I heard a sniffle.

It came from Alison.

"What's wrong?" I asked her.

"I'm scared to sleep over,"

she whispered in my ear.

I gave Alison a hug.

"Sleeping away from home

can be kind of scary," I said.

"What would a real princess do
to make Alison feel better?" I asked.

"Protect her from villains!" Rose said.

"A princess faces her perils
with strength," Molly said.

Alison still looked scared.

"I know!" I said.

"A real princess would have

a dragon to protect her!"

"Close your eyes," I said.

"Unlock the magic kingdom!

What do you see?"

"Nothing," said Alison.

"Listen!" I said.

"Do you hear the dragon
walking in the enchanted forest?"

"That's your dad walking down the hall,"
Rose said.

"Breathe!" I said.

"Do you smell the odor
of dragon breath in the air?"

"Oh, excuse me," Molly said.

"I just burped!"

"Wait!" I said.

"Don't you hear the loud beating

of the dragon's heart?"

"That is my heart," said Rose.

"I've never seen a dragon before!"

"Now open your eyes," I said.

"The dragon is here!

It is pink and it is breathing fire.

Look how spiky its tail is!"

"I see the dragon!" Alison said.

"It is sparkling in the moonlight."

The dragon smiled.

"She will protect us," I said.

"What do you think

the dragon's name is?" Rose asked.

Alison yawned.

"Can I tell you in the morning?

I'm so sleepy," Alison said.

"Goodnight, Princesses of Pink,"

I said.

"Goodnight, dragon," we all said.

Outside, the dragon winked.